HUNGER
THE SECRET DIARY OF A STARVING
TEENAGE GIRL

BY

SHELAINE MCKEE-WORKS

WE READ BEAUTIFUL COMING OF AGE STORIES ALL THE TIME FILLED WITH COMPELLING CHARACTERS DISCOVERING WHO THEY ARE, AND ALL THAT LIFE HAS TO OFFER THEM

THIS IS NOT ONE OF THOSE STORIES

Dec 18TH

I just got this journal!! it was a gift from my English teacher Mrs. Hayes, a real gift! Not an assignment. She gave them to the entire class, they are really composition notebooks, but still it's the best Christmas gift I will be getting this Christmas. As I left her class with my journal in hand she said to me...you have lots to say behind those wise brown eyes, you should write and write often. Little does she know, or I dare say care, my wisdom comes from my hard life. At 15 years old I am wise beyond my years but not for the right reasons, I feel old, I feel tired, I feel scared, but most of all I feel HUNGRY.

Dec 19th

Christmas vacation, most kids look forward to Christmas vacation all year long, but we are not like most kids. Christmas to us does not mean anything, we do not even celebrate it. It has nothing to do with being dirt poor it has everything to do with my dad. He has never allowed us to have anything to do with Christmas NO reason NO debate just NO. So, Christmas to us is not a good thing it means no gifts, no tree, no decorations, no holiday music but most of all it means no school lunch for over 2 weeks. It's starting again I must go

LATER....... Same old thing screaming, crying, crashing of glass (must be that big mirror it's the only thing left unbroken in that damn room) a loud thump against the wall and then silence that eerie silence. (all the sounds of my childhood) I got the little ones to sleep finally after telling a story about a faraway land where there are Christmas trees and gifts and music. A big Christmas feast to top it all off, I swear by all that is left of me I will give them that someday even if I must escape with them to a faraway land.

Dec 20th

It's been a long day and I'm tired. I did all the housework (as usual) and Thomas raked the leaves and looked after the little ones and mama. Mama stayed in bed all day today (her reward for taking it from dad) she is absent again not speaking. I used to ask her why she took it and she always said to keep him off you kids.

Mama was put in a mental ward for a week once when she was found wondering the streets (after a fight with dad) she didn't even know her name. The doctors said she was depressed and sent her home (probably because she had no insurance) I sometime wonder if they had kept her and helped her if she would have taken us away and saved us from this hell. I do believe she was and is depressed but she is so much more damaged than that body and mind, she barely speaks anymore mostly she just stares off into space as if she is only a shell of a person. I also believe after being hit in the head so many times she can never function right again. I learned to face it a long time ago mama can't help us because mama can't even help herself. If my dad reads this I AM DEAD.

Dec 21st

I'm sitting by my window trying to write by the glow of the street light. It's quiet tonight (for once) dad passed out on the couch. We had 2 cans of condensed soup to divide between the 4 of us as, mama won't eat, and dad never eats when he drinks he says it kills his buzz. So, we had more than we are used to, and the little ones are fast asleep with happy tummies. I look out the window at Mrs. Johnsons house next door. She is and has been our beacon of hope for 12 years, I see her tree all light up (SO BEAUTIFUL) Even though she hates my dad (as does most of the free world) she always has a smile for us kids along with secret food and love. She is the angel next door. I bet her house is warm and smells of something baking. I bet there is even Christmas music playing. Oh, what I'd give to be there right now, but dad put a stop to us having anything to do with her (he even threatened her) My dad is ONLY a man of his word when he is issuing a threat and Mrs. Johnson know that he would kill before he lost his precious check. Which reminds me it's getting close to time for a case worker visit. (it's supposed to be surprise visits, but we are so used to them that we predict when they are coming) so I will be cleaning my ass off tomorrow and making sure the little ones are properly bathed. I will just have to tell her that mama is sick. (again)

Dec 22nd

I don't know how writing about my life can help me escape my life but somehow it does. I look forward to writing every day sometimes twice!! This journal is turning out to be a real God send. I had no idea how writing things down can clear them up in your head. I don't know why I'm writing or to whom I am writing it to, but I know I must write.

I am getting really worried about food, there is next to nothing left in the house (as usual) We only had a few crackers and some peanut butter today. Thomas and I gave ours to the little ones (we can handle the hunger better then they can) Food stamps will be a little late this month due to the holidays. Mrs. Johnsons flashlight is my only hope. My dad is a monster! Right before he went to threaten Mrs. Johnson he went to the local library and used the internet to get the addresses of all her children and grandchildren (EVIL prepares well) She knows he will make good on his threats, she told me once they always get out of jail eventually. I know she fears him and I don't blame her but I'm still not sure why he threatened her, I suppose it's because he doesn't want anyone close enough to our so-called family to find out how bad things really are.

She knows things are bad she just doesn't know how bad. Like she knows dad beats mama, but she has never actually seen it just the after effects, but she does know for sure that he does not hit is kids (YET) she made me promise to tell her if he ever does. Till then, she gave me my own personal beacon of hope a flashlight. I am to turn it on and put it in the window seal if there had been no food that day. (understand I do this as a last resort as I know Mrs. Johnson is not some rich women she is a 62-year-old retired nurse and probably lives on a fixed income) the next morning there is always a bag of food behind a loose plank in the fence between our houses. Tonight, I put the flashlight in the window and go to sleep and dream of what will be there in the morning. God bless Mrs. Johnson and God help us, I pray.

Dec 23rd

I snuck out early this morning and got the bag and crept back up to our room. Little Marie was smiling she knew what was in that bag, at 8 years old she is also wise beyond her years. I carefully separate out the food into 4 portions of course I always give the little ones more than me and Thomas get. There were fresh rolls and peanut butter sandwiches, pretzels and brownies. Mrs. Johnson is always careful to pack everything in paper towels and to take out of any store-bought packages, so we can flush the paper towels and throw the bag away, no evidence she says, Mrs. Johnson is a clever lady, I know we would have starved by know without her.

Dec 24th

Christmas Eve (for other people) I wish I had something for the little ones and Thomas (who does not like to be included in "the little ones") We have never had a tree. We have never sat on Santa's lap. We have never been to a Christmas parade. Oh, how I wish we could all go to bed all excited tonight barely able to sleep because we just can't wait till morning. Understand I am not writing from experience, but I have seen enough movies and listened to the other kids at school talk to know what Christmas should be like especially for good kids and we are good kids. I must go dad is calling…. God help me

Later: BIG SURPRISE!!!!!!!!!!!!!! The food stamps came, and dad is taking us to the grocery store!!!! I used to make grocery list, but dad would get mad and make me throw them away. He gets all these prepackaged foods that cost so much more and does not last long enough but he is never open to suggestions. My dad has a system (he thinks he's so smart) he has these people (real scum) who let him buy their food on our food stamps and then they pay him a little less then the total!!! He uses the extra money to buy booze. Those people all know he has 4 kids and a wife, but they don't care they just want their little discount.

But WOW something AMAZING did happen……. I guess dad got the holiday spirit (NOT) something came over him, (maybe it was the BIG BOOBED bleach blonde standing next to the ice cream?) he told us loudly (in the voice he reserves ONLY for the case worker) kiddos get you a gallon of ice cream. (she looked at him like he was Father of the Year!!!) She said, oh how sweet, BUT you will never get them to bed in time for Santa with all that sugar in them (SHUT THE HELL UP BITCH WERE HUNGRY) I wanted to tell her. For a moment I thought dad was going to take her STUPID advice and I could see the disappointment wash over Marie and Brad's faces, but dad just said, Hey you're only a kid, once right? while giving big boobs a wink, he motioned for us to get the ice cream we grabbed it before he could change his mind.

When we got home he put the whole gallon in the middle of the table and said grabs some spoons and Merry Christmas. He laughed as he went off to enjoy his whiskey. We ate it all! There is so much in a gallon that we all got to eat without me and Thomas having to worry about leaving more for the little ones. It was so wonderful to feel something we haven't felt in longer then we can begin to remember......maybe even never!!!

. a strange feeling........ a weird sensation......dare I say it?........FULL
MERRY CHRISTMAS

Dec 25th

Christmas day (again for other people) Mama finally got out of bed. She came shuffling into the kitchen she sat in a chair and stared out the window all day. I know she is gone forever trapped inside her own mind. Her body is so broken down, she moves slowly and winces with pain when she sits or stands up. Dad got mad at her just sitting there and told me to take her back to bed. I put her to bed like I always do when she is like this (which is most of the time now) I tuck her in like a child. But a strange thing happened as I was leaving the room she spoke it was barely a whisper, but it seemed like she understood what she was saying as if she had momentarily returned. She said I'm so sorry,

Looking at her stunned I realize she is worse then ever and will never come back to us. Why would she even want to come back to a life like this? Sometimes I would like to just check out for a day or so too (God that sounds awful) What I mean is sometimes I just need to rest t my brain for a bit from all the stress and worry of my life. Is this why some teens do drugs or drink?? To escape??

Dec 26th

Dad is on a real bender, mama has not eaten in days and there actually IS food in the house. Marie has a cold and we have no medicine. I fixed her some soup today so at least she had a good meal. Even when there is food in the house we MUST NOW get permission from dad to eat it. NEW RULE!!!!! He says it's, so he can keep track of it, so we don't run out. (REALLY) I must go Marie needs me.

Dec 27th

Mama won't wake up!!! Brad woke me crying, Mama won't wake up!!!! I jump out of bed and run to her bedroom. I had to catch my breath when I saw her and suddenly everything seemed to go in slow motion.....little flashes are all I remember.....call 911.....Mama????Dad screams........Police cars....red flashing lights......questions from strangers.......everything goes blurry....I'm spinning.........can't catch my breath..........Then a sinking falling feeling.........I am being held by Mrs. Johnson. How can I feel so much love when I'm feeling so much pain at the same time?

Dec 28th

Mama's gone????? Is this real or is it a nightmare???? It's both my life IS a nightmare.

Dec 29th

Everything is so still. Very much like the storm is over and now there is no wind.

Dec 30th

No funeral just a short private graveside service. I stood frozen next to the hole where they lowered my mama into the ground. It was so final. I knew she loved us, she was just no longer able to express that love. It became the LITERAL

MEANING of unspoken love. I know her pain is over. I wish I'd had flowers to place on her grave.

A memory comes flashing back to me as I write this, it washes over me like warm sunlight yet at he same time gives me cold chills..........I am very small........maybe 4 or 5........I am picking yellow flowers......somewhere I don't know where........I have my little arms full of them..........I can smell the sweet smell of the flowers....I give them to mama.....she smiles......Is this the last time I saw her smile????? She said, the only thing prettier in this whole wide world is you.

Suddenly I here Amen, I was brought back to reality. Time to leave. Leave mama behind forever. I felt grief tugging and my heart....... I also felt ANGER.

Later:

I can't look at dad because I know he killed her, he has been killing her for 20 years she just finally helped him finish the job that's all.

Jan 1st

A new year? Can I take another one?? The house is so quiet, too quiet. It all seems so unreal even though we have been watching mama die for years. But nothing prepares you for when it does happen. The little ones are all cried out for now. I held little Marie all night while she cried fighting back my own tears I must be strong for them. Thomas is doing the same with Brad. Will Thomas and me ever have our own time to grieve???? Or must we hold back forever?? Can we hold back forever??

I never understood why people brought food when someone dies. I never thought that people who were grieving could eat much, but then again, we are most definitely not NORMAL people. There has never been this much food in our house EVER, we have never had 3 meals a day, much less 3 good meals. Most of what was brought to us will spoil fast, so we will not be able to make it last, which means something AMAZING eat all you want. Eat all you want?? All you can eat?? That is something so foreign and unknown to us we can't even imagine it. So, we just stand and stare at the food, we hesitate, as if the food will have bit us first. How can you fear something so basic and want It so bad at the same time??? (Maybe because we know how much we will like it and we also know we'll probably never get it like this again) I got tears in my eyes watching Marie and

Brad being able to ask for more and GET IT!!! We have never had second helpings. When they saw my tears, I lied and told them I was sad about mama, little Brad said (and this really tore me up) Don't cry Sis mama would be happy to see us eat this much. I had to excuse myself from the table. I went to the bathroom. I let the tears flow......I have never cried so hard so violently in my life (and believe me I have cried A LOT).....I cried for mama....I cried for Brad....I cried for Marie....I cried for Thomas...and finally................I CRIED FOR ME.

Later: A few words about tears. Where so they come from?? How can you have so many inside you??? Do you ever just run out??? What is it like to have a day without tears OR the need to hold back tears??? Does everyone need to cry as much as me???? Or are they better at holding their tears back??? Can I learn to hold mine back better??? Will that make me strong???? So many questions about tears NO real answers.

Jan 2nd

Marie is sleeping peacefully in her bed alone. (I hope her dreams are a sweet as she is) I am finally back in my bed, holding her while she cries, and sleeps has kept me somewhat sane the past few awful days. Last night she said, too tight, in her sleep and I realized it was holding her so tight I was almost hurting her. That made me realize also how scared I am of losing her, of losing all of them. I fear if things don't change I will lose them all one by one. Life without them is not a life I wish to live.

Jan 3rd

I am still in a shocked trance....

Later: I am coming back around but still I am shaken to my core. I will try to write this down, I need to write this down to try to make some sense of it. Last night when I was back in my own bed writing I got cold I pulled the blanket over me a shoved my feet under my pillow. That's when I felt it touch my toes......the letter!!!! Since last night was the first night I have been back in my own bed I realize IT HAS BEEN THERE ALL ALONG since the night mama died. She must have put it there that night as I slept.

My dearest daughter,

I am not sure how long I will have my mind here with me today to write this I am sorry I can't save myself or you kids. I am broken I am a burden. Save your brothers and your sister. Its wrong to ask you this but Fight. You come from a long line of strong women the chain just broke with me. Now you must take your place find your strength and fight. Please forgive me. I love you.

The letter was dated over 2 years ago!!!! Had she been planning this all along???? How many times had she tried to write this letter in her brief moments of some form of sanity??? How many attempts did it take her to finish??? Did she forget she had even written it 2 years ago??? Did she just find it??? Did finding it make her act on it???

Jan 4th

Tomorrow is the first day back at school how will I get through it???? I need Mickie. She is the only one that will understand my pain.

Jan 5th

The first day back at school was a blur, people just assumed my trance like state was from losing my mom and that was part of it but most of it right now is the letter. It has consumed me. Why does it consume me?? Why did she write it to me?? Why did she leave me this burden to bare?? Is it really a burden or just my cross to carry in life?? Does she really trust me to save my family?? Does she really think I'm that strong?? Am I being called strong by a crazy person??? Since no one has ever called me strong before, do you have to be crazy to believe I am strong?? So many questions have sent me into a downward spiral (Am I losing my mind now?? Is it genetic??) I feel like I am slipping away from everything and everyone, sounds seem softer, colors seen dull, I feel detached, Am I really here?? Where the hell is Mickie???

Later: I am not here....... I am not there.... but the most TERRIFING REALIZATION just came to me

IAM NOT HUNGRY!!!!!!!!!!!!!!!!!!

Jan 6th

Mickie is back at school today. Mickie is my best and only friend. We have been friends for over 4 years since we first met, it was an easy pairing at our school kids stick together based on classifications poor with poor, rich with rich, jocks with jocks, stoners with stoners, smart with smart...and so on.... But poor-drug-free-non-athletic-weirdos? There seems to be only 2 me and Mickie. Mickie waits outside for me in her too thin coat, she is shaking in the wind. Since she was not at school yesterday (I dare not ask why just yet) I feel a great flood of relief that she is here now because I need her. She grabs me and hugs me tight, tears flow from our eyes. Mickie does not say much but when she does it always means something so profound I know to pay attention. She simply says stay strong you have 3 good reasons to. The stay strong part both comforts and haunts me, but Mickie is right I do have 3 good reasons Thomas, Brad and Marie. Me and Mickie have always had a lot in common but know we have one more thing in common.... dead mothers.

Later: We ate the last of the food people brought tonight.

Jan 7th

School sucked today. I can't pay attention. I got called to the counselor's office for a "TALK" (yeah right what a joke) All I could do the whole time was stare at her candy jar and pretend to listen to her rambling on and on and on. The counselor is not here for kids like me, I'm simply a requirement to meet with occasionally as part of the welfare program. She is just following procedure to update my file since my recent family "loss" as she puts it. I can tell by her total lack of eye contact she does not care I'm just more paperwork for her. I'm sure she has me filed under NO POTENTIAL meaning I am not college bound. She has no clue that college is the least of my worries when I don't even know where my next meal is coming from.

Later:

Only oatmeal and a few crackers for supper tonight, I'm glad I saved an apple and a juice box from lunch today. Thomas saved an orange and a cookie. Mickie said she would bring food from her house for us tomorrow. We will have to hold out till tomorrow, the case worker will leave us alone for a while since we are grieving, and dad knows this, so he is not going to do anything about the food situations (or lack thereof) the hunger is growing worse than ever.

Jan 8th

Mickie came through for us, her backpack was stuffed. 2 sleeves of crackers, a half a jar of peanut butter, 3 cans of potted meat, a can of spam, a can of tuna and to chocolate bars. Thank god for Mickie. Mickie gets plenty of food at her house but seldom has an appetite due to all the LOVE she also gets at her house. Love from her sick perverted step-brother Chaz. She rarely talks about it and I know not to pry with Mickie, but I can tell she is reaching her breaking point. Ever since the day she went to her dad and told him what was happening she has changed. Her dad told her boys will be boys and she was making too much out of it. Now Mickie is growing more and more restless and I just know she is going break, I wish I could help more but Mickie is not one to ask for help and she knows I can barley take care of myself and that I have 3 more to care for. That's what I mean when I say Mickie and I have so much in common, we both carry huge burdens and are trying to find the strength to save ourselves. The question is Can We????????

Jan 9th

I need to make some decisions and fast. Mickie asked me today just how much do I weigh now? (I don't know, and I am afraid to know) My jeans are starting to get baggy again and she noticed how thin Marie is getting too. We have always been bad thin, we never get bigger just taller. But is guess when you add grief and stress and loss to the regular daily hunger all bets are off. The taller we get the thinner we look. I don't know how it is that no one in a position to really help has never noticed or maybe they have and choose to look the other way. I must come up with a plan to save us. Am I strong enough? Can I save us? How will I do it?

Jan 10th

I woke up this morning and realized dad never came home last night. Is this a good thing or a bad thing? It's Saturday which means lots of laundry to do so I won't be able to write much today.

Later: Dad came home around noon…. he seems…. I don't know? I can't explain how he seems. No word seems right except maybe…….absent.

Jan 12th

I did not have time to write yesterday but something is up. I got up last night to use the bathroom but when I switched on the hallway light nothing happened, so I just felt my way to the bathroom. When I got up this morning I saw the lightbulb was missing from the hallway. I got that sick feeling in the pit of my stomach. It can't be? Where did he get the money? I mean I know It's cheap but…. This is not what I need right now (not that I ever need this shit) Oh God no! I can't take anymore.

Later:

Dad has been in his room all day. The light is on I can see it under the door from the darkened hallway. He is talking to someone, but there is no one there. Is he talking to mama? I decide to take the little ones outside. I know it's freezing but better to bare the cold then to face dad if he's doing what I think he's doing.

Jan 13th

Mrs. Johnson saw us outside yesterday and discreetly handed us a bag of food over the fence, she said we were much too thin. She is very concerned about us. I hide the food in my room. The last thing we need is dad going off on Mrs. Johnson. She is so kind to us, were so lucky to have here. When I look at her I know there is a God, even if it seems he has lost out address.

Jan 14th

I pray my gut is wrong. Dad has been awake for 3 days now and has had nothing to eat. He has been holding up in his room. Even though we have enjoyed the peace I know it comes at a huge price. The lights stay on in his room constantly (this is not a good sign) I fear the worst.

Later:

The worst is here. I can smell it! That strange mantellic smell. I know that smell. I know the fear that only that smell can give me. I know what happens to kids who live in a house with that smell. I know what it all means. Dad is not alone in that room. Dad is with the MONSTER.

Jan 25th

I have not written in a few days. I must watch dad like a hawk I have to keep the little ones outside as much as possible and cannot risk writing out there and dad seeing me through the window if he ever got his hands on this journal all hell would break lose. If I'm going to do something now is the time. My dad and the monster do not mix. Once it consumes him it will come for us and consume us all. That's another awful thing about the monster it never hurts only the user. There is a damn good reason why they call it the monster.

Jan 26th

I skip school today and go to see Mrs. Johnson. I know it will be ok because the school will not be calling since our phone is disconnected (dad didn't pay the bill again) They probably won't ask me much either when I return, since I'm grieving. Walking past her house to the bus stop I tell Thomas and the little ones to try to save a little from lunch today. Then I duck behind the fence and into Mrs. Johnsons house. We talk for a long time. Trying to come up with a plan for our salvation. I told her maybe I could hold out till I was 18 and get a job and take care of the others. She said that was very noble of me, but it would never work, they will never give a teenager custody of 3 children. I guess I knew that. We threw around ideas and then she said there was really nothing left to do except to call for help and I know she's right. But I also know what will happen.

Jan 27th

I thought a lot about what Mrs. Johnson said about calling for help. But I know we will be separated. I also know there are laws about closed adoptions, so I may be able to find Thomas since he is older and has less of a chance of being adopted, I also know he will be looking for me too. But I may never find Marie or Brad and I will not chance losing them forever. I am so sorry if I am making a huge selfish mistake. But I cannot lose my family. Their all I have, and they need me. After all I have been their real mother all along. How can I chance losing them? They are my children, my brothers, my sister, my family, my best friends and my whole life. I must think of something and I will. I read the letter again there is no real need to read it as I have it memorized. How does one find their strength?

Jan 28th

Dad was out of his room and gone when I woke up this morning. I used that time to confirm my worst fears. I searched his room, Right out in the open on the nightstand I find it (I was right) (though I wish I were wrong) the lightbulb all black from use. (guess he's still too cheap to buy a pipe) I search more just for kicks being able to go though his things somehow give me a sense of power, as if I am the one who is one step ahead for a change. I find 178 dollars in his old work boots (old from age not use) I decide to take 11 dollars, not much I know but the amount is small enough he will maybe just think he miscounted. If I'm lucky the monster will just make him forget how much he had to start with. The monster can make you forget a lot. For most users they forget that they once had a conscious. Did will never forget that because he never had one to begin with. Where did he get 178 dollars????

Jan 29th

I took the 11 dollars to the store and bought a big box of raisins, a box of crackers (god we are sick of crackers) 3 cans of potted meat, 2 cans of franks and beans, a small box of coco and a bag of marshmallows. At least the little ones will have something sweet. Hot coco even if it is made with water instead of milk plus it will help with the cold weather (being outside so much lately) to have a warm drink. This is the coldest winter I have ever felt or maybe it just feels colder because I am so thin. I am now officially thinner than I have ever been. I have been giving most of my share of food to the others. The cold presents another problem it will be harder to keep the little ones outside and away from dad and the monster. I've still been racking my brain to come up with a plan and still nothing I need to eat so I can think straight.

Jan 31st

Mickie was not at school again today I am worried. I was thinking about showing her the letter. I know she cares and would want me to, that's what friends are for right? But how can I dump my problems on her when she has so many of her own? Why am I always worried about being selfish? Have I not always been there for Mickie? So why do I feel bad about letting her be there for me? I know the answers to these questions, I feel sorry for Mickie, and she would hate me if she knew that. Mickie does not want any pity form anybody.

Later: I know I must eat more I am weak and still losing weight. But every time I put food in my mouth I feel selfish, like I should have given to Thomas, Marie or Brad. I suppose this is a nearly lifelong habit that I must learn to break. I cannot save them and myself if I am to weak to fight. I need my strength. I am not selfish. As a matter of fact, I am as unselfish as a person can be! Just look at how long I have denied myself food, so others can eat. That is amazing to have the strength to go without food a basic human need. (Wait................ did I just say strength?) I did.

Feb 2nd

It's getting harder to find time to write as everything is moving so fast. I feel like I am standing in the middle of a crowded room screaming at the top of my lungs and no one can hear me. Will I end up like mama? That is slowly becoming a huge fear to me. I think maybe it has always been on of my deepest and darkest fears, having a mama like that is one reason I fear, but also remaining sane in the life I must live? I wonder if it is normal to have these feelings? Strange thoughts? Unrealistic fears or wait are they unrealistic? I can't think straight right now. I think I'm losing it. Maybe it's just low blood sugar. I must eat.

Feb 4th

Yesterday dad invited some scumbag over named Jack. He smelled awful, and all his teeth were rotted out (I'm sure from Meth) he was around dads age 45 or so, he had sores all over his face and he cursed with every breath. Within minutes they were both so high on the monster it was scary. Thomas and I decided to take Brad and Marie outside. They feared the monster man. As we were going out the door dad made us all come and say hello to monster man. The way he looked a little Marie made my skin crawl and I nearly got sick to my stomach when that bastard told little Marie to come and sit on his lap! Marie hide behind me and monster man said, well if you won't maybe your sister will? Dad was laughing the whole time......sick........ dirty.... bastards.

Feb 5th

Our case worker Ms. Taylor stopped by today. Dad was gone we told her he was out buying a few groceries. Well you could sure use them, she said, when she saw the fridge and the pantry. She asked us if we had enough to eat. (seriously!! Does this bitch not have eyes? Can she not see we are just flesh and bone?) I suddenly felt rage building up inside of me and fast. Ready to burst. I'm tired of all the lies. I'm tired of protecting dads check. I'm tired of pretending. I'm tired of watching us all waste away. I may not have the nerve to tell her the truth, but I will not lie anymore. So, I just remained quiet and enraged and did not answer her. Then as if she could read my mind she said, you all look thinner then the last time I saw you. (Oh god was some of my thoughts out loud?) then she said, that's only been a month that's fast weight loss, are you sure you are getting enough to eat? Again, I could not speak. Suddenly It was like I was in a fish bowl and she was outside asking these questions, they were just muffled sounds vibrations around me from an eerie distance. I was afraid if I opened my mouth the water would flow in and I would drown trapped in that glass bowl.

Later: If Ms. Taylor had any sense at all and knew how to do her job than the bitch would not need to ask questions would she? We are just another case number to her it seems (story of my life) guess it is a good thing I had my moment and kept my mouth shut.

Feb 6th

Mickie is pregnant!!!! She is only 16 years old.

Mickie's dad will not listen to her and called her a whore!!! She cried so hard on my shoulder saying, what am I going to do? Her dad loves that piece of shit Chaz like the son he could never have way more than could ever even begin to love Mickie. You see Mickie was a big disappointment to her dad because she was born a girl. (hence the name Mickie) After Mickie's mom died within a year after Mickie was born her dad took up with and married some stripper (who also already had a child she did not want) when the stripper took off she left Chaz behind just gave him to Mickie's dad, and so it began from that day forward Chaz was the golden child, adopted as soon a possible and loved unconditionally. Mickie's dad told her she was lying about Chaz and he would here no more of it. He told her to get the real father to pay for an abortion and never mention it again or get out of his house.

Feb 8th

Mickie unwillingly and not knowing what else to do went to the women's health center today I skipped school and went with her. I had to be there for her. Mickie does not believe in abortion (not even in a case like her own…. rape) But she needed to know her options and the health of the baby. I waited with her but oddly enough she seemed calm when they called her back she even insisted on going back alone. (I know why now she was ashamed of how long she had kept this a secret) so needless to say she is way to far along for an abortion and out of a home. Mickie told me she'd rather be homeless then to be forced have an abortion anyway. She said, I was forced to have sex which resulted in a pregnancy and I'll be damned if I'm to be forced to have an abortion too. Mickie wants for find a good home for her baby with loving parents. A good home with loving parents? Like either one of us would know what that is or how to find it.

Feb 9th

Mickie's dad made good on his threat and kicked her out. But he was shocked when she reached under her bed and pulled out a suitcase. She looked him square in the eyes and said, I was just leaving anyway. She is headed for her aunt's house in North Carolina. (the one her dad never speaks to) her aunt once told her, Mickie you are the only thing I have left of my dear sister if you ever need me.......... Mickie couldn't remember the rest, it had been 6 years since she had spoken to her aunt, 6 years since her aunt and her dad had a family feud. She just hoped and prayed her aunt's words were still true and that she could track her down. I'm writing this while Mickie sleeps here next to me. She had nowhere to go so I snuck her in through my window for the night. I know it is risky, but dad never comes in our room (that I know of) and she will leave a first light long before dad wakes.

Feb 10th

Mickie just left. I walked with her down the block, so we could say goodbye out of sight of the house. Chaz did give her 65 dollars told her to get on a bus and never come back (asshole) but he's in her past now and she never has to see him again. I held her close hugging her for what seemed like forever and too fast at the same time. I wish I could freeze time and stay in a moment for as long as I need to learn to accept it before I must move on. She told me to stay strong and she made me promise I would.

I know once dad finds out she is pregnant he will call her a whore and never let me speak to her again so, I gave her Mrs. Johnson's address and phone number to contact me as soon as possible. And I made her promise. She did. I watch Mickie walk away. She walked in what seemed to be slow motion. It was as if we were somehow physically attached by an invisible cord coming from my chest close to my heart. The further she got away from me the stronger the pain in my chest. Is this what it feels like when a bond is broken? Right before she turned the corner and disappeared out of sight she turned and blew me a kiss. Then she was gone. I got that sudden sinking feeling in the pit of my stomach again, the felling that it was the last time I would ever see her. I dropped to the ground and cried holding my chest till the pain became dull. I feel numb inside.

Feb 11th

 School was awful without Mickie (not that anybody asked about her or even cared) My grades are slipping again. It is so hard to concentrate when you are always hungry. Teachers always say eat a good meal before a test (do they not have a clue?) Dad always insist that we keep our grades up above average to good, so he can use that as an excuse to our case worker. You know (the kids are doing well in school) the simple fact that this excuse works is sad.

Feb 12th

Back to crackers and oatmeal for supper there is nothing else left. Since dad is still running with the monster he does not even care that the food stamps have been deposited into the account. (I know they have been for some time because it is the 12th of the month!!!) we need to go shopping. We need food. My jeans are so baggy now. I had to borrow a belt from Thomas just to hold them up. He told me I had to start taking my full share of the food. He has even been trying to give me his share. But I refuse to eat much when they are hungry, even though I know my body is growing dangerously thin. Tonight, I will have to use the flashlight.

Feb 13th

Dad is getting much worse the monster has now fully consumed him body, mind and soul. He stays on a constant high. Again, I wonder where does he get the money? At least so far, he stays in his room and leaves us alone.

Later: What the hell?? Dad came out of his room and was acting in a way I have never seen him act before……NICE!!!!!! I've never seen him like this before EVER!! He came to our room! And he told me to get that grocery list I'm always bitching about and he would go to the store. I grabbed paper and pen and started writing as fast as I could. (I knew this nice thing can't last long) I put lots of bulk items on the list dry beans, pasta, potatoes, rice and lots of staples like flour, sugar, and meal. I even put instructions on where to find them in the store. (I just hope he follows the list) I also put brands to and not to buy to save money. I know not many teenagers would know this stuff, but I am not like other teenagers, when food becomes so much more then pleasure or requirement, but instead the difference between life and death, you learn all you can learn. When I was 13 we went a whole 5 days without food. When hunger strikes you that hard you become obsessed with food. Kids at school that won't eat lunch piss me off! Just thinking of families sitting down for a meal and kids complaining about not liking something pisses me off! Worst of all is those little skinny emaciated anorexic bitches at school (starving themselves on purpose!!) they piss me off the most! Dad sure is taking a long time at the store. I'm getting worried.

Feb 14th

Valentines Day. (I don't feel the love) But I do have a nicely stocked kitchen! Dad followed the list and even bragged about my list and how he got so many bags full of groceries for so little money! I am pretty sure this is the first real compliment from him I have ever received. He said I was to start making lists from now on. But now I know the real reason……. more money for booze and now of course meth. I guess the reason it took him so long last night to get back with the food is because he had to get up with some of his scum-of -the-earth-grocery-discount-customers and of course now his meth dealer! I guess he needs more cash now if he's going to do both booze and meth. I know if he stops following my lists that it will mean less food due to the monster. But at least we have food for now I need to build myself back up I am getting weaker.

Feb 16th

Getting harder to write every day. I'm so tired. Dad stayed up all night again (and is still up) playing loud music. He is really on one this time, guess he scored big the other night. It was all I could do to stay awake in class today. I haven't slept in

2 nights. Study hall was much harder because you must be real quiet and when your sleepy that is a recipe for detention. (Dad would really go off on me for detention never draw attention) so for the sake of staying awake I listened to the whispers of conversions around me. Two skinny girls were talking about the diets they were on. I can't even begin to imagine having so much food available to me that I had to make myself NOT eat it. One of them said, my dad tried to order me the super-size meal! Can you believe that? The other girl said, No way!

Do they not have any clue as to how lucky they are? What's wrong with them? They need a reality check. I must have been staring with my mouth hanging wide open or something because they shut up and looked right at me. One whispered to the other (In a voice she was sure I could here) What do you expect? She's trash. Then the other one said. I know but she's still thinner then us. Wonder what her secret is?

I stood up walked right over to them both and said (in a voice loud enough for everyone to here) Food stamps don't buy super-size meals! I'm of the welfare diet!

I walked out feeling like I had accomplished something. (Exactly What I accomplished …. I do not know)

Later: Brad had to stay in a recess today because he fell asleep in class. We all need a good night's sleep.

Feb 18th

Dad call me to his bedroom door and told me to fix him something to eat today. He seems almost happy! Is this why he does drug? To be happy when there is no other way to be naturally happy? He is for once leaving us alone, keeping the utilities on, plus the new agreement about the grocery list. Maybe we can bare this a little while longer. I hope. Wait did I just write the word hope? Since when did I become a hopeful person?

Feb 20th

I have been very busy cooking lately. Bulk food and staples take longer to fix than easy fast prepackaged foods. Don't get me wrong, I don't mind at all I love to cook. And I believe I would still love it just as much if my situation was better. I love the smell of a meal cooking or something sweet baking. I love setting the table. I love the feeling of accomplishment at putting an entire meal together and then serving it. Most of all I love knowing that for now each of our plates will be filled with hot delicious food!!!!

Dad is still in that room (when he's here) he goes out a lot too. We are starting to get a little peace and are feeling physically better by the day. Marie and Brad are all over the place jumping and playing they have so much energy with 3 meals a day. I still miss Mickie something awful. I wonder and worry about her and the baby all the time. I have so many questions. Did she get to her aunt's house? Did her aunt take her in? Is the baby healthy? I heard that piece of shit Chaz is dating 3 girls at the same time! Both from different schools. Chaz goes to a private school! Public school was not good enough for the golden boy. Sometimes I think I should say something, protect other girls, as he will graduate this year and be off to victimize college girls. But I'm sure no one will believe me just like Mickie's dad did not believe her. Or did he? And just not care?

Feb 23rd

I am not getting to write as much as I would like to lately, but it is for a good reason. With dad still gone a lot we are getting so much time alone to do things (almost) like a normal family. Things like sitting down and playing board games together. We have never had time or energy or even enough peace to do such things before. While we have this precious time, I love to pretend we are a perfect and normal family. And as I am the eldest I am watching the others while our mom and dad are gone out to a romantic dinner. I know most teenagers would be irritated to have to babysit for that reason. But I would love it.

Later: Dad just got home (here we go again) he just turned the music up wide open. So much for sleep for us tonight. I wonder why the neighbors do not complain? This is ridicules to live like this. What was I thinking? I knew the peace would not last. Why do I give myself permission to hope? I can smell that eerie metallic smell again.

Feb 26th

Mrs. Johnson gave me a letter from Mickie!!! I was so excited I forgot to even say thank you, I ran to my room and ripped it open as fast as I could. She didn't make it to North Carolina. She only had enough money to get as far as Texas? (that's not that far??) Anyway, she thought she could hitch a ride, but nobody picked her up, so she gave up and spent a couple of nights in a bus station. She met a guy there. Patrick 21 years old from Huston Texas. He offered to buy her a cup of coffee and something to eat. After he heard her story he offered her a place to stay for a while. She is living with him and they are together as in a serious couple!! She said she is truly in love, that he is an amazing guy. He told her he would raise the baby as his own. This makes no sense to me. Mickie has never been the "fall in love" type (probably because of what she has been through with Chaz) she is a real skeptic when it comes to love! She does not trust men!!! What is going on????? Patrick who??? No last name??? I am worried to death. Living with a guy? In love? Just met him? I examine the letter closely, no return address?? She gave me no phone number in the letter. I have no way to reach her. Why would she not give me any contact info? Maybe she does not want to be found for some reason? There is that sinking feeling in my gut again. God let it be wrong.

Feb 28th

Today is my 16th birthday. Happy birthday to me. Dad does not even know when any of our birthdays are. We never celebrate the either. Mama once said, when you get older they will just be another day to you anyway. But still a girl's 16th birthday is a milestone in her life, right? I have seen girls drive up at school in new cars for their 16th birthdays. I would just like to have cake I can share with Thomas, Marie and Brad.

My Fantasy sweet 16 Birthday: (Every girl's dream)

A party with lots of food and a BIG pink cake with 16 candles on it. A healthy happy mom all dressed in pink for the occasion. A dad in slacks, button down shirt and a pink tie. A few good friends, the kind with lives that are also happy. A high school football star, popular, super cute that my respectable parents approve of and will be taking me on my first unsupervised date the following weekend. And finally, a candy apple red convertible with a pink bow in the driveway.

OK, I have officially lost my mind. This is not even wishful thinking it is total insanity. Let me be more realistic.

My fantasy sweet 16 birthday:

A cake.

March 1st

I'm doing better in school my grades are up. Probably due to the fact I'm not always so hungry. (How long will that last, I wonder) I still miss and worry about Mickie. Nobody at school talks to me. I have that detached feeling again.

March 2nd

Dad is throwing a cussing fit!!!!!! Our case worker Ms. Taylor called to set up an appointment for him to have his case reviewed. (this is always a sign you may be losing your check) I'm not real sure why dad gets a check anyway I'm not sure how it all works. I just know dad won't work. He tried forever to get a check for disability, he claimed post-traumatic stress syndrome from the army. I mean how stressful can it be to do LAUNDRY! He never saw anything to be stressed out about. Like I said I'm not sure how he got on the welfare to begin with, but it proves my theory something is wrong with the system.

March 3rd

Dad is gone to the meeting.........I am scared. If there is anything that will set him off completely. This is it.

Later: Dad came home. He was screaming about how we must have said something to Ms. Taylor when she did her last inspection. He said, you all started it and you all are goanna fix it. He started barking out orders left and right. House clean top to bottom......us clean body, hair, teeth.... food cooking......grades up....no trouble what so ever or we'll be sorry. (I believe we already are) We all said yes sir and went to follow his instructions.... everyone except Marie. She just stood there looking at him. I told her to come on. Dad said, no it looks like she has something to say. (this is where things got bad) I told her to come on again, but dad said, no he bent down and got right in Marie's face and said, you got something to say? Marie was frozen in fear and stood very still and kept quiet. So, dad said louder, you got something to say? When Marie still didn't answer, he blew up! The next thing I knew he had Marie over his lap hitting her so hard over and over. This was not a spanking on the second hit he balled up his hand and started hitting her with his fist, he was literally beating her! I saw red! I I leapt forward and grabbed his arm in mid swing and pushed him backwards with all my might. Thomas picked up Marie. He stood up looked deep into my eyes, but I stood my ground (for a moment) he swung his fist hit me right across the face, I saw back. When I woke up Thomas was cleaning my blood off the floor, Marie was in the corner crying, Brad was holding a wet cloth for me. (dad was nowhere in my blurry sight) I sat up slowly, spit out more blood, and a tooth came out hitting the floor. Thomas was quickly at my side I said to him, never again.

March 6th

Thomas woke me this morning and said I have something to show you. I drug my bruised and sore self out of bed and went with him to dad's room. Thomas said dad left early this morning. He opened the bedside drawer and there inside were needles and syringes. This is for H (Heroin)

All bets are off now!!!!!!!!

March 7th

Swollen, bruised and sore, oh so sore. How did mama take this? I can't believe how much damage one punch can do. I'm swollen and bruised across the entire lower half of the left side of my face. I am missing a lower side tooth, my tongue is cut, my neck is like whiplash, my right elbow is bruised, my right hip is bruised and sore and there is a knot on the right side of my head. I guess I underestimated what fighting back would be. Still I would do it all over again because it stopped Marie's beating. Poor Marie has bruises all up and down her backside. Thomas has been taking good care of us. Brad is still in a shocked state. He will barely speak at all.

Thomas keeps saying he sorry over and over for not stepping in he feels like he failed us. He told me he wishes he was strong like me. But I'm not strong. Or not strong enough.

March 8th

I have not been back to school since the fight. I can't let anyone see me like this. But Mrs. Johnson did as I carried out the trash. She broke down crying, but it was not a sad cry, it was a mad cry. A real mad cry! Then she came stomping around the fence like she owned the place. She screamed, where is he?! She had this fire in her eyes that I have never seen before on her or on anyone! All the sudden I could not imagine this woman being afraid of my dad or of anyone or anything on this earth! I told her he was gone for now, she to me to come with her, put her arm around me and led me into her house. She sat with me and held me silently for a long time as we both cried.

Oh, how I have wanted to go to her so many times and tell her everything, I know she has been waiting for me to. But is was afraid for her and for us. Has living with fear made me so weak I cannot even ask for help? Especially when it's being offered? She told me, made me promise that if he ever hit us kids to let her know but instead I have lain in my pain and sorrow for days. Suddenly I pulled away and said, I'll be right back. I went to my house and got the letter. It is time I shared this burden with someone else. Someone I trust. Someone wise. And Mrs. Johnson is all those things.

March 9th

Mrs. Johnson read the letter and once again she held me silently and we both cried. Then she began to speak to me, she told me, my mother was not well and even though she did not want to judge her, it was wrong of her to dump such a burden on me. Then she said... (and the is the part that got me) No one in this world knows a person better than their mother, so that part about you being strong is something you are going to have to tap into.

We went over several options (again) calling the authorities. Running away. Sticking it out. Even killing dad! But all the options meant the separation of my family. I told her how Brad had stopped speaking and Marie was afraid of her own shadow. They would never make it without me. Mrs. Johnson said it was her civic duty to report abuse. I begged her not to or at least to wait until I could figure something out. She thought about it for a few minutes, I could tell she was really struggling with it. Finally, she said, ok but, if I so much as suspect any more physical abuse I will call the authorities, better to be separated if it means your all safe. I asked her, what about dad's threats against you? She said, I'll worry about that, besides those threats were only valid to me when kids were not being hit. Now the game has changed.

I went home and thought about all that Mrs. Johnson said. And I wondered how someone like me with life long bad luck could have a Mrs. Johnson next door. I fixed supper than I tried to do some housework, but the pain and soreness are just too bad I need to rest. I decided to take a hot shower to help with the pain. When I got out of the shower feeling a little better, I wiped the steam from the mirror and stood there in shock!! As if I was seeing my injuries for the first time!! Maybe the bruises had darkened throughout the day? I looked horrible. Beaten, broken, pathetic. And if that wasn't enough to wake me up I suddenly pictured Thomas, Marie and Brad with these injuries and that was the final nail in the coffin. I AM DONE!!!!!!!!!!!!!!!!!!!!!!!!!!!!!!

March 10th

I waited this morning for dad to leave and I marched right over to Mrs. Johnsons with my new-found determination. Together we made the decision to call for help. I know what that means but, I will be 18 in less than 2 years and free to find them. Mrs. Johnson said she will help me keep track of them she still has friends from the hospital and hospitals work with social services, she was sure some of the people she knew could help, or at least knew someone who could. And then we came up with a plan..........

I will call for help but first, Thomas and I will be sure to memorize Mrs. Johnsons address and phone number, plus the names of all her kids (got that idea form dad, strange how his evil plan has helped with this plan) Marie and Brad are too young to remember so Mrs. Johnson is going to buy 2 teddy bears, one each for Marie and Brad. She is going to open the backs put all the contact info inside and sew them back up. I will give them to Marie and Brad and explain their purpose. Like I said, Mrs. Johnson is a clever lady. This plan will be hard on everyone, it's not what any of us wanted, I will have to work hard to prepare them well and make everyone understand that we may have to be apart for a while. But I will promise them we will be back together as a family. I just wish I could tell them when for sure. God give me strength.

March 11th

I will make the call from Mrs. Johnsons house in a few more days. We need the teddy bears and Thomas and I need to memorize all the info well. I also need to prepare everyone more and reassure them this is the best option. This must work. Will it work?

March 12th

Mickie is dead......

March 14th

I'm still crying. My heart is shredded. Everything has stopped. Even my hunger. For the first time in my life I can't eat.

Later:

Greif is so demanding on the mind, body and soul. You cannot escape it. It is like trying to run from your own shadow.... impossible to do unless the sun goes down on you. God don't let the sun go down on me.

March 15th

There is no bearable way to find out your best friend is dead. The way I found out makes me feel so out of touch with reality. I wonder if being out of touch with my reality is such a bad thing? Dad made me go to school due to the case workers review. When I walked in the building they all turned my way. Some stared, some looked away and lowered their heads, some turned back to what they were doing pretending not to see me.

At first, I thought it was my face. I thought they could see traces of my bruises (even though I tried to cover them with mama's old make up which is too dark for my completion) Can they see the bruises? Are they staring at my too dark makeup? Did they find out about my dad hitting me? What is going on? At my school all I have ever been is overlooked.

Then a do-gooder girl named Jena came up to me. Jena said, I'm sorry if you need anyone to talk to I'm here for you. (I had for idea what she was talking about other than my face) I knew Jena always tried to help people but never me. Finally, I took a deep breath and said, talk to you about what? She looked stunned (there goes my gut again) she said, you don't know do you?

I said, know what? (louder than I should have) she said, you better come with me and started leading down the hall by the arm, towards the office. I said, just tell me already. She didn't say anything. A rage started building in me (is she screwing with me?) I stopped right in the middle of the hall, spun her around, I got right up in her face and said, tell me now!

She said, Mickie's gone. I breathed a sigh of relief (really! They are just now taking notice that Mickie is gone?) I said, yeah, I know, I got a letter from her she's doing ok. (like you ever cared I wanted to add but did not) then Jena teared up (I knew this was bad) she said, no you don't understand, Mickie died.

I backed away from Jena…. I think she was still talking……. I couldn't make out the words……I couldn't breathe…. I needed air…. I needed to get away……everything was fading……. I needed to escape, I needed to run fast and escape the pain. This time I needed to outrun the pain. So, I ran, out of the school, down the streets and I did not stop until I reached Mickie's house. Where the pain was waiting for me, you cannot outrun the pain.

March 16th

I still don't know why I ran to that damn house. It was never a home for Mickie, the stuff that happened in that house killed her in the end. I don't know why but I just stood there for over an hour yesterday staring at it. No one was there. No movement, no sound, almost like it was dead too. On my way home, I saw a newspaper in a machine and my heart stopped (again) there was a guy standing there looking at it too. I asked him for 50 cents, he looked at me (noticing my tears) said nothing and handed me the change. The headline on the front page.

Local pregnant teen runaway's body found on Texas roadside.

The article had no real details, just that her body was found by a truckdriver on the side of highway 6 in La Marque Texas. She was 5 months pregnant at the time of her death. And her death appeared to be foul play. They had questioned a suspect and a full investigation was underway.

But I know they never fully investigate poor runaways. I may never know what happened to Mickie and her baby but, I figure it had something to do with that Patrick guy. I can't just blame him, I blame Chaz and her father too. Seems as if every time I lose someone there is always someone to blame. Mickie never hurt anyone, yet she endured so much. Will I end up the same way? Will Marie? I remember Mickie's last words to me.........Stay strong.

March 18th

Mickie was laid to rest today. (laid to rest) I hate how that sounds even though I know she was tired from all that life had dealt her. I waited until everyone was gone and I went and sat by her grave, I cried. Cried for Mickie, cried for her baby, cried for myself. I cried, I got mad, I even for a moment laughed. I don't understand how the grieving mind works. How can you feel so many emotions at one time and then become so numb you feel nothing? It was an unexplainable wave of multiple emotions flooding over me. I felt crazy in a sane way, as if crazy is my normal and sane is me pretending to be normal.

March 19th

It is interesting how tragedy make you remember so much. I think maybe you realize you need to try to remember all you can just in case you are next. I sat at Mickie's grave again today for a good long while. Talking to her as if she could her me. Can she? I feel like she can. I told her about our plan to call for help and how I was trying to stay strong like she told me to. I told her how much I missed her. I told her I did not know what was going to happen or when I would be able to visit again. I told her I loved her. when I stood to leave, a light gentle breeze found me it felt so much like one of Mickie's gentle hugs. I know she heard me and I know she is telling me she loves me too.

Later:

I was walking home today after visiting Mickie's grave and I got to thinking, it's strange how the mind wonders off. Its' even more strange when you think of something and suddenly it has an all new meaning. Like Mickie's house, it was never a home. So now I understand why Marie (who first started talking at 2) used to say house instead of home. (as in, I go house) I would tell her it's home, but she still called it house and still sometimes does. It struck me that even at 2 Marie knew the difference between a house and a home.

March 20th

With all that has happened the past few days, my plan to call for help has been delayed. But not anymore. It is time. I am going to the payphone Mrs. Johnson told me to use at the mini mart three blocks down the street. Here I go...god give me strength.

Later:

I did it!!!!!!!!!!!!!!!!!!! I called the social services and they put me through to a case worker. First, she asked why I was not at school? (bitch) I answered by saying, well I thought saving my brothers and sister, not to mention myself, from starvation at the hands of my heroin addicted meth head abusive father, might be a bit more important then algebra! (wow, where did that come from? Dare I say, strength?) She said ok, ok, calm down and let me get some information. When I hung up I knew that this was a life changing moment.

March 21st

Marie and Brad have their teddy bears (they love them) I have prepared everyone. We all know the plan. Now we must act cool and wait. I hate waiting. Waiting is always the hardest part. Tick tock, tick tock, tick tock.

March 22nd

A knock at the door today sent my heart racing, (already? I thought) dad answered the door and it was Ms. Taylor! Dad smiled acted all sweet, invited her in and offered her something to drink. (wonder if she would like whiskey? Or hey Ms. Taylor how about a hit of meth? Or maybe heroin?) dad called us all to the living room. As we all walk into the living room, dad turned to Ms. Taylor and said, they were studying, dad bragged to Ms. Taylor about how good we do in school. Then Ms. Taylor started her questions about the usual stuff. Has dad been looking for work? (not) Have we bought any new appliances or furniture? (not) Blah. Blah. Blah.

This is a regular visit!!!! They did not take me seriously!!!!! Did my attitude piss them off on the phone???? Did I screw it up??? Mr. Taylor checked the pantry, looked around to make sure things were clean, checked that the heaters were working. Than she asked us kids how we were? (right in front of dad of course) Dad butted in bragging about how well behaved we are and how I have become such a fine cook. How the boys are growing like weeds. (what?) And just how much he misses mama (cue tears in dad's eyes) .... (cue gag in my throat). Is she really buying this act???? But then she said, I thought they were a bit thin the last time I was here, and they don't seem to have gained much if any. Now I know my dad and trust don't belong in the same sentence, but, you can always trust my dad to put on a good show. He said, with total sincerity, (cueing more tears) they haven't had much of an appetite for a while now, since their mother passed. He went even farther (lying) about how he had tried buying cookies and ice cream and even candy just to get us to eat. (P-L-E-A-S-E) If Ms. Taylor buys this act she is a total idiot!

Later:

Ms. Taylor is a total idiot.

March 23rd

Still nothing. I am freaking out. Are they not coming to help us? Did Ms. Taylor stop them? Is there anybody out there that will help us?

March 25th

There is a lot to write today:

It happened today!! A person from child protective services showed up. A woman named Ms. Baker and she had a cop with her. She inspected the house, the food, and looked for signs of abuse on us. She found no evidence. Dad kept acting all panicked like he could not bare to lose his kids. (when I know it's his check he can't bare to lose) The women said, they had reason to believe there were drugs on the premises. The cop searched and searched and guess what? Nothing!! (dad must have hidden his stash well or took it somewhere else since his case is being evaluated) Ms. Baker talked to each of us kids separately. She told us whatever we said was totally confidential. I told her he hit me and Marie (but with no marks left on us I know it would be my word against his) I told her about the drugs (but I know with none found again, it was my word against his) I could see this going nowhere fast. After talking to all of us and to dad she said there was no evidence of drugs or abuse. Of course, dad asked her where she got her information. She told him that it must remain confidential. Dad asked if there was anything to worry about (he even cried) He kept saying, I can't lose my kids, I can't lose my kids. (pretty good performance, he must be practicing) he added, they have just not been the same since their mother took her own life. (more crying) He spoke through streaming (fake) tears, she was not well for a very long time. I could see the sympathy in Ms. Bakers eyes for him. (he was winning) So after all the searching, questions, and dads Oscar winning performance. She said, since the children seem well (hello can't you see how thin we are you stupid bitch) And since there is food (I think she is attracted to dad really stupid bitch) And since there is heat (yep no wedding band I checked) And since they are doing well in school (oh so, since we are smart that makes it different?) I can see no reason to proceed any further except maybe some unscheduled future visits. Dad won again. But guess what dad? I am not through yet.

Later after Ms. Baker and the cop left.

Dad was in a fit of pure rage. He wanted to know who turned him in. He kept asking us, interrogating us, then I saw it in his evil eyes, he had an idea who turned him in. He said, it was that old bitch next door wasn't it? Dad bolted out the door ready to unleash a world of hurt and the target was Mrs. Johnson. He went right up to her fence and started kicking it and screaming. You bitch get your old ass out here!!!! Get out here bitch!!! You don't turn me in bitch!!!! They didn't do anything you bitch!!! Ha Ha Ha bitch you get that? Come on out and I'll give you more!!! You lost bitch!!!! Nobody messes with my family (check)!!! Come on out!!! Come on!!

Dad shut up for a few seconds to listen. Nothing! Dad was thrown by the silence, which made him even madder (as if that were possible) He then started around the fence to her yard. He was going for her back door! Then Mrs. Johnson broke her silence. At first, I couldn't believe it was sweet Mrs. Johnson, but then I remember that look she had and her eyes when she saw my bruised face. Oh yeah that's Mrs. Johnson. She broke her silence in a big way, she kicked her screen door plum off the hinges! It went flying of the porch and hit the fence with a loud crash. Dad stopped in his tracks.

She came stomping out of her house war face on, carrying a double-barreled shotgun under her arm, she raised it, cocked it and took aim right at my dad's head.

She said, (in a strangely calm voice) Take one more step and it will be your last and nobody's loss!

Then she went off, I have not heard language like that in all my life (and I have heard a lot) I heard a slew of F-bombs and apparently Mrs. Johnson thinks my dad changed his name to sorry bastard. Nor have I ever seen my dad that scared (not even over losing his check) he was shaking. Mrs. Johnson made herself crystal clear.

She said, listen up and listen good I'm only going to say this once. I did not turn you in, but if I do it will not be to some lady in a business suit with a rent a cop in tow. It will be to the county coroner! You fuck with me or mine again and your dead! You got that sorry bastard? Dad just nodded. Mrs. Johnson seemed even more pissed I though she was going to shot him anyway. She said, you answer me when I speak to you dammit!! Dad said, Yes mam. She nodded, turned and walked back into her house and softly closed the only remaining door. We all just kind of stood around in the calm after the storm. The storm that was Mrs. Johnson.

March 26th

Still trying to process all that happened yesterday. Just when you think you have someone figured out. I think my dad met his match yesterday. Glory be.

March 28th

Things have been quiet around her the past couple of days. Dad is back in his room, he has locked himself in there I'm not sure if he is high, drunk or just hiding from Mrs. Johnson. Either way it is good to have some peace.

April 1st

First of the month food stamps are here. Dad went to the grocery store and came back mad. He could not find his usual "discount buddies" and had to spend a lot more. He can't risk a visit from social services without plenty of food in the house. That means a lot less for is habits. Since his habits went from booze to meth to heroin, it cost a lot more and I know he cannot go without all of it now. He is shaking, trembling and sweating a lot. He is very ill and moody. His eyes are like that of a wild animal, I can tell he needs a fix. Or he might explode on us.

April 2nd

I got up and got ready for school. Dad is in the bathroom throwing up bad. We used the kitchen sink to wash our faces and brush our teeth and went off to school. I got that bad gut feeling again. School was a little better people stopped staring at me. I guess Mickie's death is old news now (for them). I got called to the counselor's office again today. this time about Mickie (took them long enough) I told them I was dealing. Again, I understand this is just procedure. I am not important enough to them to try and save. I saved some of my lunch today. A granola bar and a pudding cup. I know we have some food at home right now, but we have none to spare and with dad in a bad way I had better be prepared. The truth is no matter what the situation I will probably always save food out of habit.

April 3rd

Got home from school and dad is still in a very bad way. I think we better all stay in our rooms and be very quiet, so I will just fix supper and we will all eat in our room.

April 4th

I hate him. I wish he was dead. How could he????? Bastard!!!!

April 5th

Why does pain have to be such a constant in my life?

April 6th

I have stayed in bed for the past 2 days in shock. Dad didn't even make me go to school. Is this my reward for taking it?

April 7th

Am I going to end up like Mickie? These past few days I would like to just give up and join her. But I have 3 good reasons to stay strong. Mickie once told me that to me.

April 8th

I sat up in bed today and made a command decision. I will not end up like Mickie or like mama. I am leaving, and I am taking Thomas, Marie and Brad with me. I need money. I have mama's wedding band, she lost it years ago and I found it. I kept it since I knew dad would sell it besides it is not like mama missed it. I don't even think she remembered having one. I also have my grandmother's gold locket.

Later: I went and searched dads room, I found an antique pocket watch and some old pocket knives. I went to the closet to look in his old work boots for money. I thought there would be no money there, but there was!! Bastard! I hate him! In the boots I found 240 dollars!!! That bastard sold me!!!! His 16-year-old daughter!! For a fix!!! And all along he had money to buy it!!! Son of a bitch!!

Suddenly I feel sick. I run to the bathroom and throw up till all I can do is dry heave. If feel dizzy. I cry. I scream. I feel the pain all over again. I feel the shame. I feel used.

I see flashes.... I see dad handing me over to Jack......I see Jack smile.... Rotten teeth....Bad breath....Glassy eyes....I feel jack push me down....I hear dad laugh....I smell Jack......Ripping clothes...The pain is so sharp....It hurts so bad....He pushes into me....He moans....I scream....My mouth is covered...Can't breathe....More laughing.....Laughing at the virgin......Laughing at the Cherry popping...Tearing.....Ripping....Bleeding....Warm blood....Crying....Trembling... Everything fading to black.... Waking up alone in the dark.... So cold.... Broken...Dirty.... Nothing......Numb.

The bathroom is spinning I lay down on the cold tiles and the darkness engulfs me. I don't know how long I was laying on that cold bathroom floor, but I do know that I kept repeating to myself be strong, be strong, be strong. And told myself that if I ever got the strength to get up and pull myself together there would be no stopping me!

I may never know for sure where my strength came from, maybe it is from this tragedy. But when it came I was ready for it.

Later: The kids are packed and waiting at Mrs. Johnson's house. I am waiting on dad. But dad is not alone.........

April 9th

We are in an old house Mrs. Johnson owns and used to rent out. It is very old and run down. But to us it is a wonderful retreat, a safe-haven of our very own. It has a lovely working fireplace! Mrs. Johnson is going to bring supplies as soon as she can. It all happened so fast after I found my strength, but that strength turned to anger that turned to rage. I still can't believe I did it, but I do not regret it.

April 10th

Mrs. Johnson came by today and brought supplies. Candles, blankets, food and more. She helped us find firewood for the fireplace and taught us how to start a proper and safe fire. She sent Thomas under the house to find old buckets and pans (anything to catch water) for the leaky roof and tarps. She brought old curtains. She had us use the tarps and old curtains to cover the windows, so no one would know we are here. We are not to burn a fire in the fireplace during the day, she said someone will see the smoke. For daytime she brought and old kerosene heater and taught us how to use it. She said she would have the power tuned back on but that the wiring is too bad, and it would alert suspicion.

Mrs. Johnson pull me aside before she left and wanted to talk to me about what happened. But I told her I was not yet ready to talk about it and she understood. Mrs. Johnson always understands. She left saying she would return soon and would round up some games, puzzles, and books for us. We don't know how long we will be here, but one thing is for sure, we can never go back.

April 11th

We sleep a lot. I did not realize how little good sleep we got at home. We talk, plan, eat and try to think of creative ways to make the house our little special home. One thing about being dirt poor is you develop a good imagination. We make up games to play. This house is full of mystery. I have never seen Brad so alive, he is talking all the time, coming up with all kinds of ideas and full of energy.

This house feels more like a home than ours ever did. We all play a game guessing who all lived here before. I believe it was a happy young couple. Thomas believes it was a happy family. Brad believes a spy lived here undercover. Marie believes Brads story and that the spy was protecting a princess from an evil witch. (ok maybe we are getting cabin fever)

April 12th

Thomas keeps asking me what happened. I know I must tell him. How do you even start to tell someone something so horrible? Can he take it? Maybe later?

We both talk to Brad and Marie everyday (over and over) about how we cannot tell anyone that Mrs. Johnson is helping us. How we cannot get her in any trouble. We tell them this is a new plan and they must learn it. We explain to them how we will tell everyone later that we knew Mrs. Johnson had this old house, but she did not know we were her. We will say we had nowhere else to go. We will act as if we hope Mrs. Johnson doesn't get mad and press charges for trespassing. (if the authorities will buy dads stories they should buy anything) But Thomas and I worry about how we are teaching Brad and Marie to lie (and at such tender, easily influenced ages) but we know it is a necessary evil to survive.

 One thing that is working for us is that we have no relatives to speak of looking for us. Add that to the fact that we are dirt poor runaways. So basically, to the authorities we are probably not even worth the paperwork.

The part of the story that explains why we left I have not yet prepared. I know I must tell Thomas, but it is so hard for me. Mrs. Johnson already knows the truth I'm just not ready to talk about it with her. I will have to gather my strength and put my trust in Thomas and tell him. Brad and Marie will never know if I have anything to do with it, but I must tell Thomas, I will tell him tomorrow.

April 13th

I left Brad and Marie sitting by the heater. I told them to play quietly while Thomas and I had a talk. My heart pounded in my chest as we went back to the kitchen area of the house. We sat down in the floor and I immediately started crying. I gave him the short version of the rape. I told him how dad sold me to Jack for drugs (of course I spared him the details) Thomas was crying so hard I wanted to stop, but I had to continue while I had the strength. I told him about the day we left. How I sent them all to Mrs. Johnson's and waited for dad to come home. As I told him I realized I was reliving it for the first time since it all happened. All the emotions of what happened hit me head on as I spoke....

How I waited for dad full of more anger and rage than anyone should have in them. More pain than anyone should have to bare, but most of all a burning need for revenge.

I remembered when Jack came in with dad, how I let out a sadistic laugh, thinking what a bonus two for one on my quest for revenge. I told him about the aluminum baseball bat that I took from his closet. How I practiced my swing while I waited. How I watched them from the bedroom door. How they were all high and happy with themselves. How Jack was all excited to get another go at me. How sweet it was the first time. How dad laughed a sickening laugh. I remembered Jack laughing and saying. Both dealer and buyer score here! I remember how dad laughed so loudly at that sick remark. I remember how I could feel my pulse in my ears. Then I heard dad say, just don't get her pregnant, if we're going to keep this up I better get her on the pill. More laughing.

I lost it. It was time. I had heard enough. No more waiting for the right moment I just attacked. I ran up the hall, Jack was sitting in the chair with his back to me and dad was on the couch. I swung the bat with all my anger and rage hitting Jack In the back of the head then, I went for dad right across the face. Jack was out cold, but I hit him again in the head anyway, I heard dad trying to get up, so I hit him again this time in the back of the head. There was silence. In the room but not in my head.

All the years of pain, abuse, starvation, and loss all came flooding back. I saw red. It was as if it was not me anymore. I was possessed. I just started pounding them both concentrating a lot on Jack's inner thighs. He will never be able to do to another what he did to me, I made sure of that.

That's when Mrs. Johnson came in and stopped me. She took the bat from me and just stood there for a moment. I wondered if she was going to finish the job. But instead she just took me and the bat to her house.

Thomas was just sitting there staring at me in disbelief. He said, you should have told me I would have done it myself. Then he asked if I had killed them? I told him about Mrs. Johnson going back, she checked their pulses and said they were both alive. I told him how she called the cops and told them she had heard a ruckus, how she told them she saw a man leaving with a bat. Thomas asked me if the cops bought Mrs. Johnsons story and I told him the truth. I said, of course they did. He also asked if the cops were looking for us? I told him I wasn't sure that Mrs. Johnson told the cops we kids must have heard the ruckus got scared and ran off, but she was sure we would turn up.

April 14th

Mrs. Johnson came by today with an update, Jack is out of IUC and as soon as he is released form the hospital he is going to prison (for a long time hopefully) for dealing meth and heroine, apparently the cops have been looking for him for some time. I know this is sick, but I had to know about the damage I had done. So, I asked, and Mrs. Johnson told me he will never be with a woman again. Mrs. Johnson seemed pleased that I asked. Dad on the other hand is a different story. He's out of the hospital and in jail now, but he will be released soon since it is his first offence. He has not turned me in. Does he think we are even now? Is he out for revenge? Does he not remember? Is he afraid it will come out, what he let Jack do to me? Mrs. Johnsons also said that Ms. Baker came by looking for us and asking questions.

April 15th

I spent the day playing board games and coloring with Marie and Brad. It was a peaceful time even though it was filled with worry. I write in this journal even though I know how much trouble I could be in if it fell into the wrong hands. But I must write. Tomorrow I will find a real good safe hiding place for my journal. I don't know how long we can stay here or how hard they are looking for us. I know I must once again come up with a plan. Thomas said, no more plans that don't fully include him. I understand that, I have been selfish I guess taking them all away without their permission. But I knew what had to be done to save them.

Later: I got my period, one less worry.

April 16th

I just found out from Mrs. Johnson that dad is home and that Ms. Baker is back around and looking for us. She told Mrs. Johnson that we won't be staying here anymore. Not after what happened. Mrs. Johnson played dumb to get as much information as she could, since those social service people are usually so tight lipped. But Ms. Baker was really open for some reason. Maybe because she knows she could have prevented it. Or because her job performance is being questioned, or maybe she just knows dad fooled her and she is pissed. So, Mrs. Johnson asked if dad would for sure lose custody. Ms. Baker told her, a violent fight when children were present. Drugs on the premises, father arrested for drugs, sounds like enough to lose custody to me. Apparently, she and Ms. Baker had a nice long talk.

April 17th

Starting to feel like old times in the food department, but I hate to ask Mrs. Johnson for more. But I must. When I did, I even insisted that she let me pay for some of the food and supplies with the money I stole from

dad. But she would not here of it she said I would need that money later. I told her I felt bad taking her money. She told me not to worry she had put a little away for a rainy day. She went off and returned with more food and supplies and warned me not to let them get low again without telling her.

April 18th

The little ones are getting restless, they have cabin fever. I don't know how much longer I can keep them inside, but I have to. I tell them stories, play games with them and color. But nothing seems to help. I hope this all turns out for the best. I just want them to have a good life. They deserve a good life we all do. The scary part for me is that they have never asked for a better life, they seem to have accepted the hand they have drawn. When other kids get nice things, they don't even notice or envy them. They never ask for anything. Have they given up? I will not allow them to give up! I cannot bare that.

April 19th

I keep having the same nightmare repeatedly, I am not sure I can write it all down, my hands tremble when I think of it. I must write it down. I must make sense of it. I must stop the fear.

I am standing in a road...maybe a highway...it is night...it is so dark and cold...there is no movement anywhere...there is no sound...I begin to walk...at first I walk slow...then I feel the need to run...I pick up my pace...I start to run...down the lonely dark road...I run so fast...I am so hungry...I am so weak from hunger...I can't keep running...but I have to...I run until my legs give...I fall to the ground...I try to stand but I can't...I see something...I see someone...Mickie???? I crawl to her...I have to push myself to reach her...she is face down...laying on the cold pavement...face down....but I know it is Mickie....I scream her name Mickie!!!!....she does not move....I finally reach her...I touch her...she is so cold...I turn her over...her belly is round and full... the baby...then I see her face.....it's me.

April 20th

I can barely write this I am so excited!!!!!!! Mrs. Johnson came by today with the best news ever!!!!! A huge surprise!!!!! I can't believe it!!!!! It's too good to be true!!!!!

She had a letter and showed it to us. It was a letter from the state, Mrs. Johnson has been approved to become a foster parent!!!!! Showing us the letter can only mean one thing, she wants us!!!!!!!!!!! She explained that she has been working on this for a long time but did not want to get our hopes up as she was afraid she may be turned down because of her age. I'm no spring chicken, she said.

I had to ask her, would you really let us live with you? She said, you are the best-behaved kids I have ever seen and that most certainly includes my own, how do you think I got all this grey hair? We laughed, then she said, besides you kids can pretty much take care of yourselves, you always have. Then maybe one day you will take care of me, like I said I'm no spring chicken. We all had one big group laugh and hug. God bless Mrs. Johnson.

Then I asked her about dad. She said he was still at home and he was using again, there was loud music all hours of the day and night, she also said he was served papers taking away his custody and his precious check.

April 21st

Mrs. Johnson did not show up today, I'm worried. Is she ok? Did she get in trouble for helping us? Did dad do something? Did she change her mind about taking us in?

April 22nd

Mrs. Johnson came by today, she said she could not make it yesterday. When I asked her was everything ok? She said she did not want to worry me but yesterday morning all her tires on her car were slashed. She said she is almost certain that dad knows she is helping us. Then she said something that sent chills up my spine. She said there was a man fitting dads description (at a time when he was not home) outside her daughter's house, watching her little granddaughter play. That her daughter quickly brought her granddaughter inside and called the cops, the description of the man fits dad perfectly right down to a green hat he was wearing that day. Mrs. Johnson said we will have to hold off a little longer till all this blows over.

April 24th

Mrs. Johnson told us today that dad called out to her across the fence and told her what a pretty granddaughter she had. (it was him)

I cried to Mrs. Johnson telling her how sorry I am that all this is happening because of us. I told her we would get out and go to the authorities even if it meant we would be separated. She told me, Hush child, no tears. we will figure this out, just stay here for now. I told her even if it blows over there is no way the state will let us live right next door to him. Mrs. Johnson looked stunned, as if she hadn't thought of that, she walked to the window, pulled back the makeshift curtain and said, in a very strange voice, let me worry about that.

May 11th

It's been a while since I have written, but I have just got may journal back. I had it hidden in the old house just in case our stuff got searched. I know I could have still written without it, but I have grown so attached to this journal it would feel as though I was somehow betraying it. It's hard enough to write at all without the security of something so familiar that I have grown to trust so deeply. This journal has somehow been my salvation. I don't think I would have held on to my sanity without a way to vent and put the reality down in words to cement it as real so that I could accept it and start the healing process. There is no way I could have talked about all this to someone, the thought of speaking all the words I have written is completely inconceivable to me. My new reality is hard for me to come to terms with. I think I should do some soul searching maybe re read my journey so that I may come to terms with all that has happened.

May 12th

I have been reading over this journal and I am both amazed and shocked at the journey I have been on. Do I conclude this journal and start a new one with a better life to write about? I know I will always write. But am I ready to officially end this part of my life and start a new one? Have the wounds healed enough? Will the nightmares go away? Am I ready to move on? Move forward? Can I move forward? I must decide because once I write it down it will become real. Where will I go from there?

May 13th

Dad is dead. He had been dead 2 weeks now. I did not have my journal and since getting it back I have not had the courage to write about it. Till now. He died on April 29th. I feel relief, is that so wrong? It was ruled and accidental overdose of meth and heroin. He was found on the kitchen floor needle still in hand. He had been there for several days. Ms. Baker found him during a routine visit, to question him as to our whereabouts. She noticed the smell.

That's when we came out of hiding. Mrs. Johnson came up with a plan to not implicate herself in helping us and damage her foster care provider status. She had us go to a pay phone and call Ms. Baker not Ms. Taylor (she was very adamant about that) and ask for her help. Within 30 minutes the cops showed up and then Ms. Baker. We were all taken to a hospital to be checked out and then to a juvenile holding facility, while they searched for foster care. Marie and I were together, but Brad and Thomas were sent to a boy's facility.

Eventually we were all assigned to live in the foster home of Mrs. Johnson. She picked us up on May 10th. Ms. Baker said they were lucky to find foster care for all of us so fast. Than she gave me and unusual, sly almost secretive smile and a wink.

May 14th

We are all at Mrs. Johnson's or Mrs. J's as we now call her. (she said Mrs. Johnson was too formal) Maire and I got her daughter's old room. It is a dream girls room all pink and peach with matching twin beds and a window seat. (which I am sitting in now) Thomas and Brad are in her son's old room, they love it because it is upstairs and has its own bathroom. The house is so beautiful and smells of cooking (mostly baking) all the time. Mrs. J is going to have a much taller fence built, so we don't have to look at our old house. I told her not to waste money on that, as It could not spoil this kind of happiness, but she said she was tired of looking at it herself. She also said she would slowly pay herself back with the foster care money she was making now, it's her new joke, she cannot believe the state is paying her to have a house full of loving children.

It really feels like home, even if I had a real home before to compare it to I still cannot imagine it being better then this. Marie would never say I go house now.

We all pitch in and help out to show our gratitude. Mrs. J says it's like having full time live in help she feels like a queen, she tells us we don't have to do so much, but we insist. She has put her foot down on us once so far, she told us firmly, that if she found out that we were turning down chances to go out and have fun or do something we love, because we feel we owe her. She would kick us out on our proverbial asses. (of course, she said it with a great deal of charm) I heard her on the phone talking to one of her friends (I know I was eavesdropping) she was saying, I had 2 kids that nearly ran me ragged body and mind, now I have 4 kids and I am a woman of leisure.

May 18th

We all sat on the back porch last night eating ice cream cones. Everyone was smiling, laughing and just full of real honest to god happiness. I saw Brad look over at the old house for a moment as if remembering something, (my heart kind of skipped a beat) but then he went right back to eating his ice cream and laughing. Later when Marie and Brad were in bed. Me, Thomas and Mrs. J were sitting at the table talking about summer school (which we must attend to stay on track). I looked out the window for a second at the old house wondering what Brad was looking at or thinking about when he looked earlier. Mrs. J said, you all don't have to worry about seeing that place much longer, that fence is going up soon. I thought about it for a moment, and I said no way Mrs. J, don't build that fence. She looked at me like I had lost my mind. She said, excuse me? I said, you have to know where to came from to know where your going in life. Thomas agreed, he also added, who knows maybe a nice family will move in now. Mrs. J said if that was what we wanted she would respect it.

May 19th

I'm about to go to bed, tomorrow is the first day of summer school. I have new stylish clothes, a new hair cut from a real professional salon, I have new makeup, a fine backpack, new school supplies and best of all a real prepared with love brown bag lunch!

I must say it feels amazing, but it goes so much deeper than these wonderful things that were bought with love just for me. I have an inner peace, that can only be described as a shining example of god's love for me. I have been delivered from the darkness, and into the light. I am a strong force to be reckoned with, so watch out world because here I come.

TEN YEARS LATER

May 8th, 2014

Even though I have many journals full of memories now, none are as precious to me as this original first journal. So once a year I take this journal out of my special hiding place and, I read it. I do this for many reasons I cannot fully explain. But today is different, I take it out not to read It, but to add to it for the first time in 10 years.

I thought it would be fitting to have the full story all together in one place. It is also another one of those situations where must write it down to come to terms with it. Why have I chosen to do this? I have received another letter from a dead woman.

Mrs. J passed away 7 days ago, she had a long and happy life and filled our lives with love and joy. She told us once, that we brought joy in her life when she thought the best times and years were over. The same was true for us. So now exactly one week after her passing I have received a letter from her via her lawyer.

My dearest sweet girl,

Writing you this letter is one of the hardest things I have ever had to do. I hope it does not bring back sad memories of the letter you received from your mother many, many years ago. But this is the only way for me to confess to you. I pray you will forgive me. Do with this letter what you must, I will leave it up to your good judgement to decide if you want to share it with the others. I have carried this burden to my death, but I know in my heart that you have a right to know the truth. Please understand I did what I did to protect you and Thomas, Brad and Marie. And, to protect my own children.

Your father did die of an overdose, but it was administered my me. I killed your father. I will spare you the details. And considering the circumstances you will have to except that. All you need to know and that I did it, I confess, and pray you forgive me. There are some things you still do not know about your father, all said, believe me when I say it was the only way to save us all.

You kids brought more joy to my life than I ever thought possible, I will always be with you, I will always watch over you. You are all my hopes and dreams realized and my love for you all is eternal.

I love you all

Mrs. J

I do not forgive Mrs. J because there is, nothing to forgive and I have decided to not share this with anyone else, just to add it to my journal and then hide it away as I always have. There is no need to share, there is no need to forgive. I loved Mrs. J with all my heart and nothing could ever change that. She saved our lives and gave us bright futures. I will owe her for the rest of my life. How many people can say that someone loved them enough to kill for them.

We all cared for Mrs. J as she became older and frail. No matter how old and frail she became she was still our rock and we miss her every day. We have all blossomed under her care. Marie is a beautiful 18-year-old high school senior, she is an honor student and has already been accepted to a great college where she plans to study social work. Brad is a handsome 20-year-old college sophomore studying criminal science with plans to become a police detective. Thomas is now 24 he studied heating and air-conditioning at the local college and manages a small very successful company that he has plans to buy when the owner retires.

And as for me. Now 26 years old, I took my love of food and all that Mrs. J taught me about baking and became a master baker. I took a job in a large bakery where I met my husband. I was (and still am) in great demand for my one of a kind wedding cake designs. He was a jilted groom wanting to cancel an order. 11 months later he was my groom. We are now expecting our first child, a girl, we are naming her Mickie.